Sailing off to Sleep

by Linda Ashman   *illustrated by* Susan Winter

SCHOLASTIC INC.
New York Toronto London Auckland Sydney
Mexico City New Delhi Hong Kong Buenos Aires

Special thanks to Adelina ("Dee Dee"), who keeps things sailing smoothly

–L. A.

ISBN 0-439-47900-2

Text copyright © 2001 by Linda Ashman. Illustrations copyright © 2001 by
Susan Winter. All rights reserved. Published by Scholastic Inc.,
557 Broadway, New York, NY 10012, by arrangement with Simon &
Schuster Books for Young Readers, Simon & Schuster Children's
Publishing Division. SCHOLASTIC and associated logos are trademarks
and/or registered trademarks of Scholastic Inc.

12 11 10 9 8 7 6 5 4 3 2 1   3 4 5 6 7 8/0

Printed in the U.S.A.   08

First Scholastic printing, February 2003

Book design by Jennifer Reyes

The text of this book is set in Clearface.

*To Jackson, who had me
thinking of polar bears in
the middle of some cold
winter nights*
—L. A.

To Felicia
—S. W.

It's nighttime, my little one.
Climb into bed.

I don't want to sleep—
I'll go sailing instead.

There's only one problem:
Your ship has no sail.

I'm tying my boat
to the tail of a whale.

Where will you go
with this blubbery beast?

As far as we can—
to the Arctic, at least!

The ocean is icy—
you might sink your boat!

I'll ask a fat walrus
to keep me afloat.

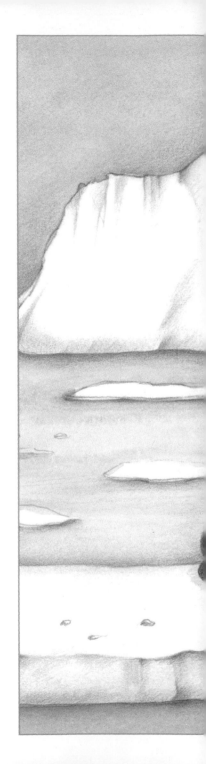

Won't you be cold?
It's freezing up there!

I'll cuddle up close
to a warm polar bear.

What about food?
You'll get hungry, my sweet.

I can make ice cream!
There's plenty to eat.

The wind can be fierce—
you'll be tossed like a ball.

I'll land on a fur seal—
it won't hurt at all.

What if you're lost?
You don't know the way.

I'll follow the tracks
of a caribou sleigh.

You won't have your playmates
to chase in this place.

I'll take on some auks
in an ice-skating race.

What if you trip?
It's slippery, you know.

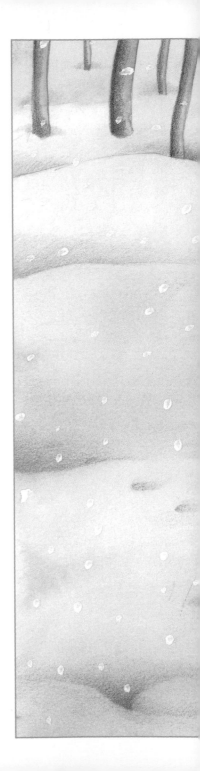

I'll ride on a moose.
They're used to the snow.

Won't you get lonely
out there on your own?

The wolf pups are friendly.
I won't be alone.

But what if I miss you?
(I already do!)

I'll find a big snow goose
and fly home to you.

And what will you do
when you're back in my sight?

I'll climb in your arms
and I'll kiss you good night.

I guess you should go—
there's a long night ahead.

Maybe tomorrow . . .

I'm ready for bed.